The illustrations in this book are hand-painted using gouache, ink, watercolour,
coloured pencils, pastels and acrylic colours.

First published in Swedish as *Alla Ska Sova* by Rabén & Sjögren in 2019
First published in English by Floris Books in 2020. Text © Astrid Lindgren. Illustrations © 2019 Marit Törnqvist
English version ©2020 Floris Books. All rights reserved. No part of this publication may be reproduced without the
prior permission of Floris Books, Edinburgh www.florisbooks.co.uk British Library CIP Data available
ISBN 978-17250-675-1 Printed in Poland through Hussar

FSC
www.fsc.org
MIX
Paper from
responsible sources
FSC® C015559

Floris Books supports sustainable forest management by
printing this book on materials made from wood that
comes from responsible sources and reclaimed material

Now that Night is Near

Astrid Lindgren and Marit Törnqvist

Floris
Books

Come now little one, it's time to go to sleep.

All the little children are tucked up in bed.

Their mamas and their papas too –

Everyone is going to sleep, now that night is near.

Even cats are going to sleep, as bedtime's nearly here.

The cows and calves are sleeping in the fields.

All the little foals, all the little piglets,

All the little rabbits, all the little lambs –

Everyone is going to sleep, now that night is near.

Even cats are going to sleep, as bedtime's nearly here.

In woodland and water, bushes and burrows,

Birds on branches and spiders on webs,

Everything that lives on earth –

Everything is going to sleep, now that night is here.

Even cats are going to sleep, as bedtime is here.

About the author and illustrator

Astrid Lindgren (1907–2002) was a multi-award-winning Swedish author and creator of many bestselling books, including *Pippi Longstocking*. Her books have been translated into over a hundred languages and are still adored all over the world.

Marit Törnqvist was born in Uppsala, Sweden, in 1964. She has won a Golden Plaque, one of the most prestigious children's illustration awards, and created many books including *Charlie's Magical Carnival* and *Wake Up, Let's Play*. Marit now divides her time between the bustle of Amsterdam and the serenity of Sweden's forests.

The pair met when Marit's mother translated Astrid's books into Dutch and the famous author started visiting the family at their farmhouse in Sweden. After her graduation, Marit was commissioned to illustrate several of Astrid's stories and they developed a close friendship. Marit visited Astrid every time she was in Stockholm and their exciting adventures included a hot-air balloon ride over the city.

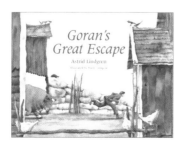